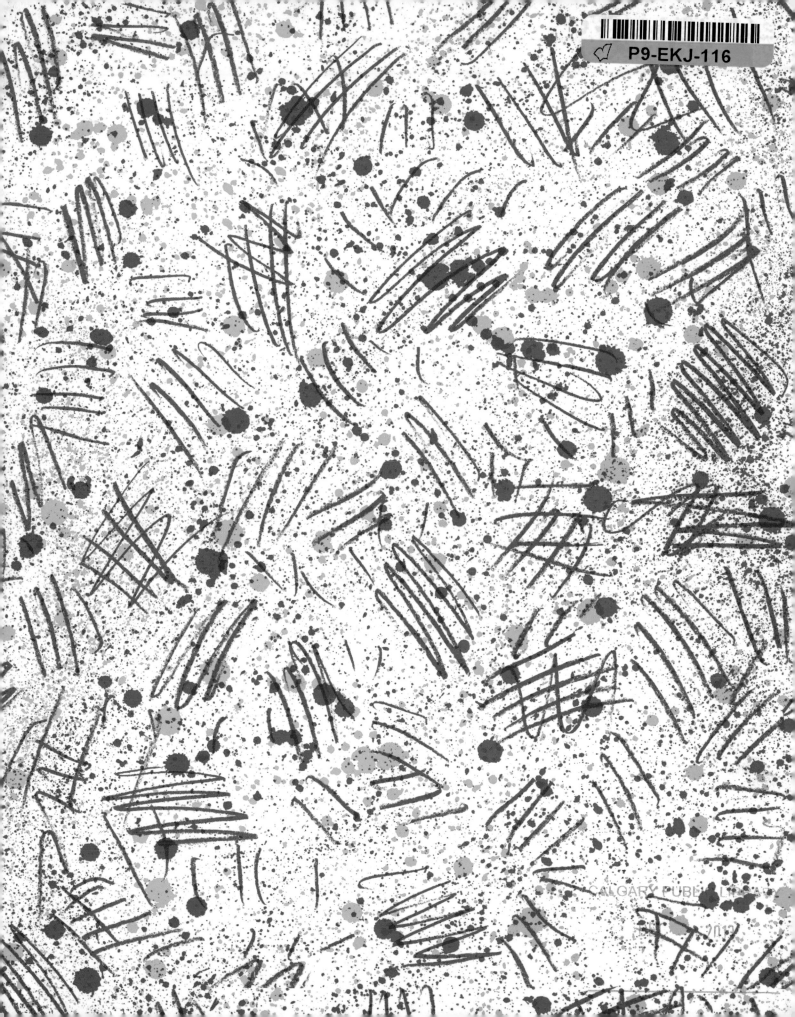

To the artist
inside of you

Copyright © 2012 Ethan Long
All rights reserved/CIP data is available. Published in the United States 2012 by
🍎 Blue Apple Books, 515 Valley Street, Maplewood, NJ 07040
www.blueapplebooks.com
First Edition   04/12 Printed in Shenzhen, China
ISBN: 978-1-60905-205-8

2 4 6 8 10 9 7 5 3 1

Visit Ethan Long at: www.ethanlong.com

Ethan Long

Scribbles and Ink

BLUE APPLE

Meet Ink...

Ink likes to paint.

Scribbles likes to draw.

They do **NOT** like each other's artwork.

Ink wants to hear what Scribbles has to say about his finished masterpiece.

Scribbles gives his opinion.

Then Ink comments on Scribbles' drawing.

Scribbles and Ink exchange insults.

Then Scribbles and Ink go their separate ways.

While Ink naps, Scribbles grabs
his pencil and decides
to show Ink who is really
the BETTER artist.

So when Scribbles takes his nap,
Ink uses his brush to prove
that HE is the better artist.

Now Scribbles has something to prove. He grips his pencil and . . .

Of course,
Ink has to
get even!

Scribbles is spooked.

The battle of the brush
and the pencil begins.

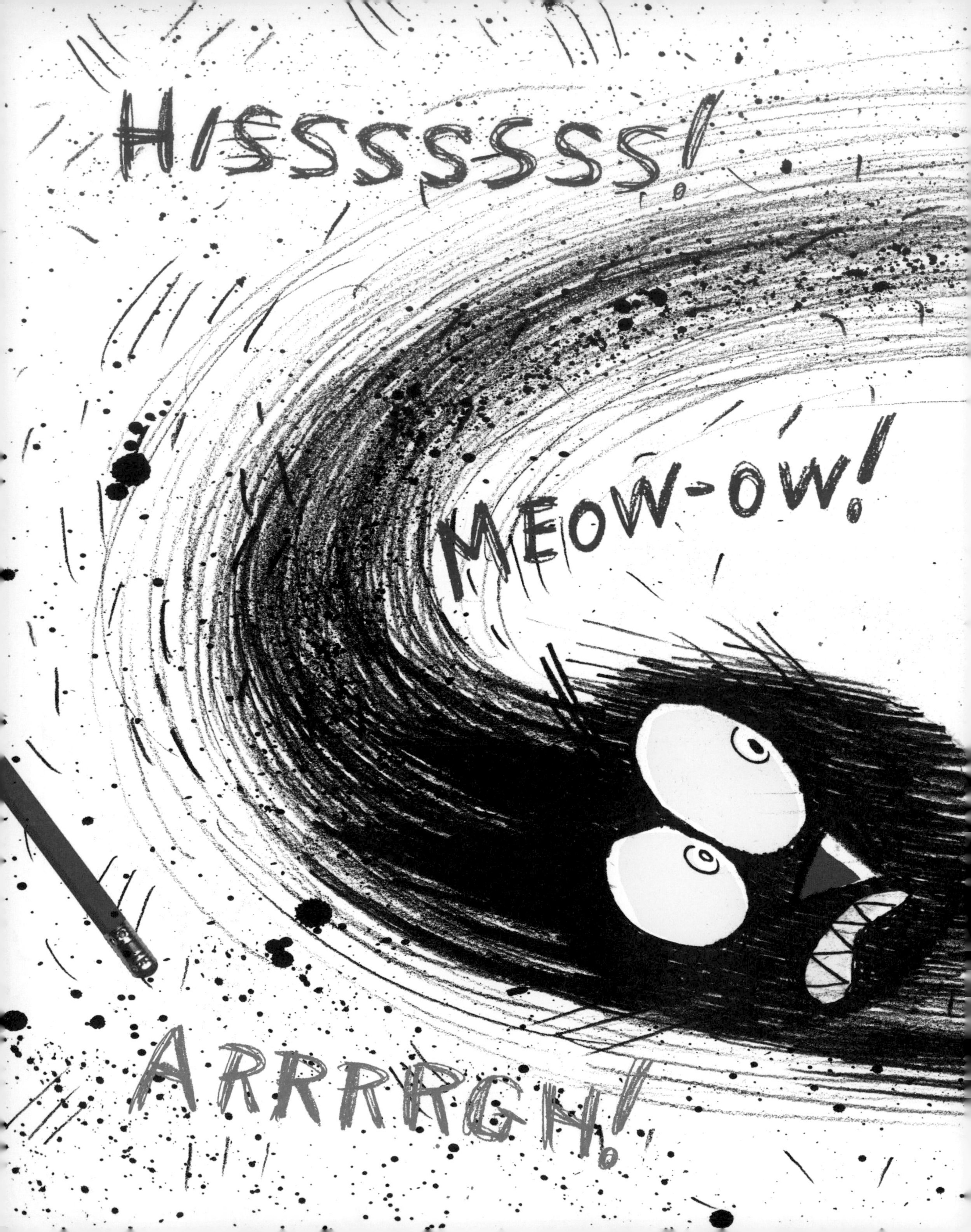
HISSSSSSS!
MEOW-OW!
ARRRRGH!

Ink Paints Scribbles.

Scribbles draws Ink.

Hmm... Interesting idea.

I LOVE YOUR USE OF LINE. WHAT DO YOU THINK OF WORKING TOGETHER ON SOMETHING?

OPEN →

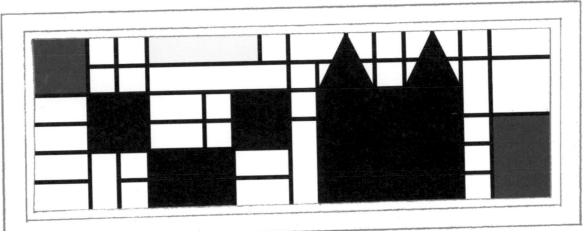

Do you know how many great artists begin? By getting out their sketchbooks and copying the pictures of other great artists who came before them. Really! This helps artists-in-training explore different styles and develop their skills.

Here are the famous artists' names and the signature art styles that inspired Scribbles and Ink. Can you guess which artist inspired each of the paintings?

GRANT WOOD grew up in Iowa and painted what he saw and knew in his daily life there. His famous painting of a farmer and his wife is called "American Gothic."

LEONARDO DA VINCI'S most famous painting is called "Mona Lisa" and shows a lady with a mysterious smile and eyes that seem to connect with those who view her.

CLAUDE MONET liked to do his painting outdoors. He pioneered an art style called "Impressionism," which uses small dabs of paint to create a shimmery image full of movement and light. He created a series of paintings called "Water Lillies."

VINCENT VAN GOGH'S art style is bold and energetic. His painting called "Starry Night" shows a church against a vivid nighttime sky.

JACKSON POLLOCK used splatters of paint to create a wild swirl of colors that didn't show an exact object, but taken altogether, still created a strong visual impact. One of his best-known paintings is "Full Fathom Five."

ROY LICHTENSTEIN often used little perfect circles of color to create cartoon-style paintings such as the one called "Grrrrrrrrrrr!" Some of his ideas came from comics, advertisements, and gum wrappers!

SALVADOR DALÍ was a Surrealist painter. This kind of art shows something ordinary that's been partly changed, or paired with something unexpected. Melting clocks appear in his painting called "The Persistence of Memory."

RENÉ MAGRITTE was another Surrealist who liked to make folks look at things differently by showing people and objects in unusual ways. In his painting called "The Son of Man," a green apple floats in front of a man's face.

PABLO PICASSO is most famous for a style called Cubism, which shows a person or thing as if it were broken up into pieces and put back together differently. His painting "Dora Maar with Cat" uses this style.

PIET MONDRIAN was fascinated with what he could create by painting with only five colors (red, yellow, blue, black, white) and by using squares and rectangles made with connecting black lines. This is shown in his painting called "Composition II with Red, Blue, and Yellow."

Visit www.blueapplebooks.com to download your own
Scribbles and Ink blank sketchbook.

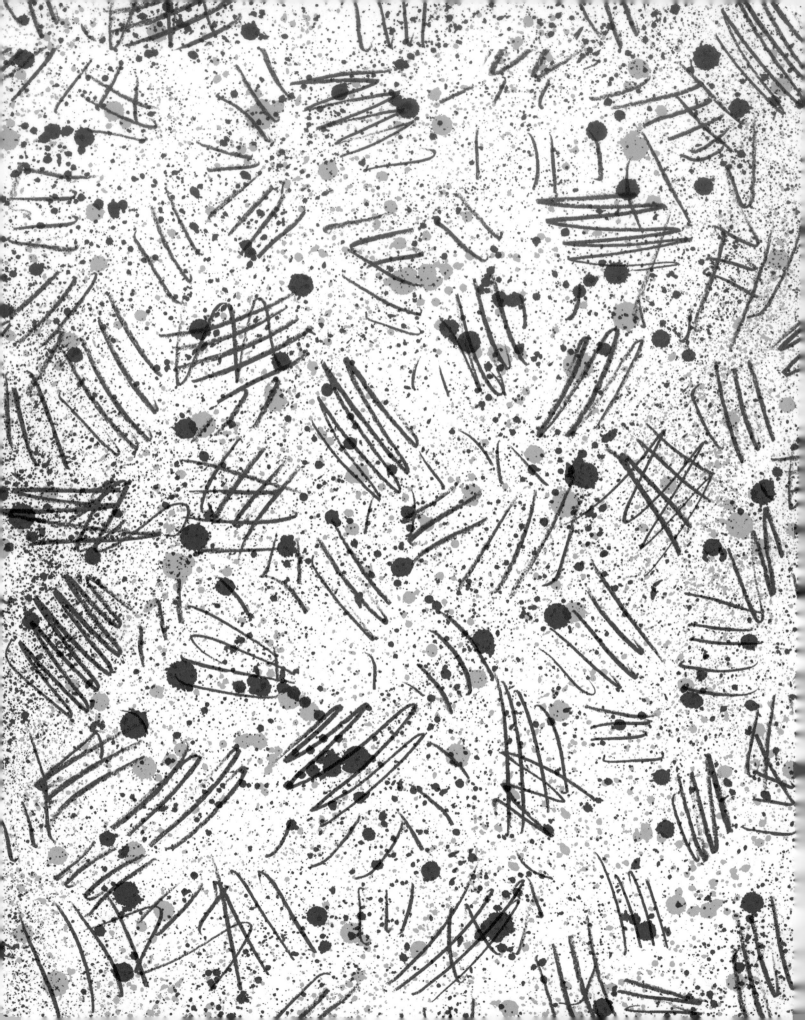